Heading Love's Way

A Next Stop Love Novelette

♥

This is a work of fiction. All of the characters, organizations, publications, and events portrayed in this novel are either products of the author's imagination or are used fictitiously.

HEADING LOVE'S WAY

Copyright © 2022 by Rachel Stockbridge
All rights reserved
Designed by Rachel Stockbridge

www.rachelstockbridge.com

First Edition: February 2022

Heading Love's Way

A Next Stop Love Novelette

Rachel Stockbridge

1

Vermont
Friday, February 12, 1993

There was only one thing Annette Lim would ever admit to hating, and it was driving on narrow, winding, icy roads. Though now, as she slowly navigated a hairpin curve some three thousand feet up a mountain, she realized there was something she hated even more: driving on narrow, winding, icy roads without a single passenger to listen to her joke away her nerves.

She was a little irritated with herself for turning Tracy down when she offered the last seat in her car. It would've meant a few hours of being stuck in a Range Rover with two lovey-dovey couples, and Annette didn't enjoy *other* people driving on narrow, winding, icy roads any more than she liked doing it herself. But there would have been friendly, cheerful people to talk to. And she was pretty sure Tracy's radio worked. She *knew* Tracy had a cassette player. So at the very least they could crank up the music.

Normally she wouldn't have thought to turn down Tracy's offer—she did trust Tracy to drive safely, and the advantage of having a working radio counted for a lot. It was just that lately Annette was getting the *time to settle down* talk. A *lot*. Almost the entirety of Christmas day had consisted of trying to extract herself from worried conversations on the subject of her singleness with her aunt and uncle—just to end up in a nearly identical discussion with her grandparents in the next room. By the end of the evening, even her parents had started hinting they were concerned about her lack of marital options.

Annette had laughed the whole thing off—it was, after all, ridiculous. She wasn't even that far into her twenties yet. Just because she hadn't dated anyone seriously since senior year of high school didn't mean she wouldn't find someone eventually. She was just busy. Grad school would do that to a girl.

Only when she'd tried to describe the incident to a few of her girlfriends a couple of weeks later, they'd all inexplicably ganged up on her too.

"Do you think you'll be any less busy after you graduate?" Heather had asked, while the rest of them nodded. Which was the precise moment that Annette realized she was the only single-person holdout in her entire grad-student friend group. In the last few months they'd all gotten themselves into serious relationships without Annette quite realizing what was happening. She must have missed the friend meeting where that particular pact was made.

"I could set you up with someone if you want," Tracy had added, far too eagerly. "There's this really funny guy in Paul's residency program who I think you'd hit it off with."

Annette had refrained from making a sour expression—Paul's questionable ability to judge 'funny' had landed her on two painfully awkward blind dates in the past three weeks—said no thanks, and latched onto the popular (at least with Tracy) subject of what Paul was up to these days. Though that hadn't prevented Tracy from pulling her aside after class a few days ago to ask her if she was sure she didn't have anyone she wanted to bring with her. They could book her date an extra room if it would make Annette more comfortable, she was hasty to add.

"I just don't want you to feel like a fifth wheel the whole time," she'd whispered, as though she thought it was insensitive to let anyone else in the women's bathroom know that Annette was on the fast track to spinsterhood. "Especially with it being Valentine's Day weekend and everything."

"I'm only going to feel like a fifth wheel if everyone plans on *treating* me like a fifth wheel," Annette said, smiling as she raised her eyebrows. "Stop worrying so much. I'm not going to mope, I'm not going to feel left out. If you guys are too boring I'll just make some ski-trip friends."

Tracy seemed mollified at that point, but Annette expected more check-ups over the weekend. Tracy had a way of mothering people which was usually endearing, but occasionally resulted in a faintly irritating insistence on "fixing" other people's "problems." Regardless of whether the other people believed they *had* a problem.

And Annette just didn't see her singleness as a problem. The men she'd liked as an undergraduate had tended toward the flighty or immature, and had an annoying tendency to start competing with Annette for "funniest partner" the second she made one joke. She got tired of awkward first dates where she had to sit through some poor fella explaining her humor back to her, and dates where the guy got so desperate to be funny he started being flat offensive instead. And she got tired of the dates where she couldn't get a word in after five minutes because apparently letting herself be silly on a date meant she didn't take anything seriously and she needed a big, strong man with a big, strong brain to make all her decisions for her. She usually made up an excuse and walked out when that happened.

Though just now—as she eased off the gas to navigate another frighteningly tight turn—she didn't think she would have minded one of those infuriating, one-sided discussions. At least bickering with an idiot about whether silliness and competence were mutually exclusive would have been something else to focus on.

Unwisely, she peeked to her right, where there was only about a yard of slushy gravel and a rusty rail between her station wagon and the steep, wooded drop beyond.

"Oh boy," Annette muttered, snapping her gaze forcefully back to the road. Her fingers were aching from her death grip on the wheel. She tried to relax. The last thing she wanted to do if she started drifting was make any sudden movements.

No matter how much she had been looking forward to the skiing and the roaring lodge fireplaces—single or no—the terrifying drive was making her wonder why she hadn't tried to convince everyone to rent a big house on a warm beach somewhere. Preferably one with no ice, no hairpin turns, and definitely no chance that a wrong twist of the wheel would send her tumbling to a painful demise.

"Stop being silly," she told herself, adopting a jovial tone that would've sounded fake to the most gullible of infants. Convincing wasn't the objective. The objective was to cut through the hushed, nerve-wracking hiss of her tires over wet, slushy asphalt. "I bet it wouldn't even be that bad, going off the road. If I'm not romantically rescued by the branches of one of these noble evergreens, I'm sure the car will just roll into a big, safe snowball and set me down gently at the bottom, no problem. Cartoons wouldn't lie to me about that."

Her nervous laugh ended in a sharp intake of breath when the station wagon hit a patch of ice and drifted. She quickly removed her foot from the gas and concentrated on not doing anything crazy, holding her breath until she felt the tires grip the road again seconds later.

Annette made a wordless unhappy noise through her nose. She couldn't be that far from the lodge, but she had half a mind to find a place to pull off until she could get her nerves up for the last leg.

But if she pulled off into one of the lookouts, she knew she would just end up sitting around until someone stopped and offered to drive her the rest of the way or call her a tow truck. There was no telling how long that would take. And she *definitely* didn't want to get stuck driving the last twenty minutes after dark.

Plus, she felt like she had to prove to Tracy she wasn't in desperate need of a boyfriend. Turning damsel in distress over a little bit of ice was hardly going to help there.

Well, if sad attempts at humor weren't helping, maybe music would. A busted radio couldn't stop her from singing.

She took a deep breath and sang out the first lines of "Total Eclipse of the Heart." She hadn't listened to the song in a while—maybe not since her obsession with it in high school—so she was making up most of the verses. She kept repeating the chorus a few extra times whenever she got to it, doing all the musical fills and tapping her index fingers against the steering wheel for the drums.

Her spirits lifted with the melody and she started feeling more capable and a little less terrified. Just as she reached the dramatic swell near the end of the song, she rounded a corner and was greeted by a sign proclaiming she had reached the turnoff for the Deer Creek Ski Lodge and Resort.

Annette broke into a huge grin, taking one hand off the wheel to point at the sign like she was belting the chorus out to her biggest fan.

Annette was still humming as she wrestled her luggage into the lodge ten minutes later. One bag got stuck on the front door, and she just about brained a passing preteen with one of her skis trying to get it free, but none of that dampened her sense of accomplishment at having arrived unscathed.

Tracy and most of the others were already hanging out on well-stuffed couches near the fire roaring in the obscenely large fireplace across the huge lobby. A young family was sitting around a checkers board at one end of the room, the boy and his mom playing a game while the dad looked on, occasionally offering hints to the kid. A few lone people were scattered around the empty seats, either waiting for friends or sipping hot drinks, their faces flushed with cold.

Another small group had stopped near the base of the staircase directly in front of the doors. She thought one of them—a guy in wire glasses with his hands in his coat pockets and his black hair standing on end—had turned to look at her as she staggered through the front doors, but when she glanced at him, his attention was on the map one of the others had just passed him. He was the only other Asian person in the room, which was probably why she noticed him looking her way. If he didn't look so miserable, he would have been cute. He had a nice sort of face and he stood with the understated confidence of a model. The slightly chaotic style of his ink-black hair just made the model impression stronger.

"Annette!" Tracy held up a steaming mug as her shouted greeting was echoed by the cluster of couples surrounding her. "How was the drive?"

"Harrowing!" Annette called back cheerfully, hitching her skis up on her shoulder and clambering toward the front desk. One ski got stuck on the mat in front of the door and almost tripped her, but she managed to kick it out of her way in time. "Are you guys still going to be down here in five minutes or so?"

"We'll wait for you," Tracy promised. "Take your time getting settled."

Somehow, Annette waved at her without dropping her skis or anything else and hefted her things to an empty space at the front desk.

"Hi," she said breathlessly, offering a big, friendly

grin to the pale clerk, who blinked at her luggage with mild alarm. Annette couldn't really blame her. Her skis were angling to turn Annette's entrance into a Three Stooges routine and she'd packed more stuff into her two heavy bags than she probably needed—she could have left most of her makeup at home, along with two of the three novels she'd brought with her. But she wasn't about to admit to an overpacking problem by making more than one trip from the car, either. "I'm with the Miller party. Annette Lim."

"Of course," the woman said, smiling quickly. "One moment, please."

"Sure." Annette tapped out a rhythm on the hickory desk while the clerk looked up the reservation. She liked the look of the place. It had that rustic, warm feel you wanted from a ski lodge. The furniture around the fireplace was chunky and comfortable-looking, and there were thick, handsome rugs laid strategically over the polished hardwood floors. A massive staircase swept up to the second floor, all polished dark wood and rich green carpeting. The paintings on the walls were of mountains and lakes and wildlife. She felt a little bad for the two bucks who had been sacrificed to have their heads mounted by the front door, but she couldn't deny it fit the ambiance. Even the huge windows looking out on the ice and snow made the lodge feel cozy. *Look at how cold it is out there*, they seemed to say. *Aren't you glad you're inside?* A decades-old echo of that Billie Holiday song: *What do I care if icicles form . . .*

For one fleeting moment an idea came to her of a warm, pleasant beau standing next to her at the front desk, chuckling as she pointed these things out. Of sitting by the roaring fire with her head on a sturdy shoulder, her fingers linked with someone else's. Of standing in the snow with her cheeks stinging pleasantly and her heart fluttering as she tilted her head back to accept a kiss—

She blinked out of the daydream as the small group of people at the foot of the stairs bustled through the front doors, and found herself making eye contact with the guy in wire glasses. Only for a split second, but she thought she saw an echo of her odd fit of melancholy in his eyes. Annette wondered what had happened to make him so miserable. And why none of the people he was with seemed to have noticed.

Which was silly, of course. They probably hadn't asked him about his expression because that was how he always looked. What she thought was misery could just as easily be a case of arrogance. Or disdain. Maybe he had second-hand embarrassment from witnessing Annette's amateur slapstick entrance.

Someone clapped Wire Glasses on the shoulder and he turned for the door, hands in his pockets, mouth set in a hard line, keeping to the back of the group.

"All right, Miss Lim," the woman at the front desk said, bringing Annette back to the task at hand. She was given a skeleton key instead of a keycard, which was suitably charming, and a couple of brochures with information about shuttle times and ski instructors and the like. Lots of things for happy, single people and their friends to throw themselves into.

Smiling, Annette listened to the welcome spiel, turned down the insistent offer to have a bellhop help with her luggage, stuffed the brochures in a coat pocket, and proceeded to huff her way awkwardly up the grand staircase to the second floor.

2

Turned out Annette didn't have the affinity for skiing she had hoped for.

She, along with Tracy and Paul, and Heather and Christine, had taken to the bunny slope at the top of the mountain at 9 a.m. sharp in order to make a crowded Saturday morning group lesson. The other two couples had abandoned the newbies for the intermediate slopes with plans to meet up at the lodge afterward.

The day hadn't started off too well for Annette. Trekking through the snow in ski boots was already difficult, and she made it even worse on herself by refusing to ask all the long-legged people with her to slow down. The lesson itself wasn't that bad. There wasn't much actual skiing involved, just a lot of *here's how you turn, here's how you stop, don't smash into a tree.* But then they *had* started skiing, and Annette's skis made it painfully clear they had it out for her. She'd managed to fall twice on her first run down the gentle slope, and her second attempt was proving to be even more clumsy.

As she stared through her ski goggles at the ice-blue sky, her chest heaving and legs aching, Annette realized it had been silly to think two days a week at the gym and plenty of city walking meant she was in shape. For her fifth fall of the day, she had successfully tripped over literally nothing. Her face was going numb, and snow had gotten down the collar of her coat and under the cuffs of her sleeves. She couldn't even laugh at herself for being this ridiculously *bad* at skiing anymore. Mainly because she was too exhausted. Partly because she kind of wanted to cry.

One of the astonishingly energetic instructors slid to a graceful stop to Annette's left and peered down at her. She thought his name was Dave. "That didn't look fun. Are you hurt? First aid isn't far."

"No, no," Annette assured him, waving a hand airily. It must have looked like one hell of a tumble if Dave had left his latest *trees plus skis equals concussion* lecture to check on her. "I'm fine. It's just that I've recently discovered my legs are, in point of fact, made of jelly."

"Sounds like you've pushed yourself hard enough for now," said Dave, not reacting to the weak humor in Annette's tone at all. "Let's get you on your feet and back to the lodge so you can rest up."

Annette was reluctant to admit defeat, but she *had* been pushing herself pretty hard for most of the morning. And, to be fair, she was using a lot of muscles that weren't often in need of a workout. She wasn't defeated, she just needed to stage a strategic retreat.

She allowed Dave to help her up and back into her skis, which had abandoned her when she took the tumble. With only a little bit of pain, she was able to ski—very slowly—to the bottom of the slope and swish herself over to a set of benches lining the path to the enclosed gondola lift that went from the lodge to the big annex building built into the mountain nearby. She stopped only long enough to wrestle off her skis and then pushed herself to her feet, ignoring a protest from her calves, and started for the gondolas by herself, skis over one shoulder, using one ski pole as a cane. She'd probably benefit more from a hot bath before lunch than anything else, anyway. And now that she wasn't flinging herself down a mountain repeatedly, she figured her legs were on their way back to having bones.

It was rough going, but she managed. The gondola going *down* the mountain was nearly empty, so she was able to sit for a few minutes. But the hike from the lift was a quarter mile of a path that was little more than packed snow. Only sixty feet from the lodge, one foot hit the snow wrong and slipped out from under her. She tried to save herself from falling by flinging out an arm, but her boot landed on a patch of ice and she went down with a yelp, shoulder-first, into a snowbank, skis cartwheeling out of her arms.

Annette struggled into a sitting position, sputtering out the mouthful of snow she'd acquired in the fall. One of her skis had landed almost perfectly vertical in the snow across the path, vibrating like a tuning fork.

Pressing her gloves over her cheeks, she started laughing. There was really nothing else to do. She'd pushed herself too hard, the archetypal overachiever, and now she was sitting on her butt in the snow without the strength to drag herself the last twenty yards to the lodge. It was a little bit ridiculous, wasn't it? She was so bent on proving she didn't need anyone to take care of her that all she'd succeeded in doing was to make herself helpless.

Good job, Annette. Round of applause.

"Hey. Are you okay?" a male voice called from a little distance away.

Annette looked up and discovered the guy with wire glasses from last night watching her closely from the lodge steps. His friends were walking toward the guest parking lot, talking loudly, but he didn't seem to be in any hurry to follow them. His black hair was still standing on end, barely tamed by whatever he used to style it, and he looked rather distinguished in his thick red scarf and navy wool coat. He also looked just as miserable—or serious, or arrogant, or whatever that expression meant—as he had when Annette arrived yesterday afternoon.

"Yeah, no, I'm fine," she said, pushing her ski goggles up to wipe tears from her eyes with one scratchy polyester glove. She wasn't sure if they were tears of pain or mirth. She chose to believe they were the latter. "No pain, no gain, right? And let me tell you, I am expecting a *lot* of gain tomorrow."

Wire Glasses frowned, but not unkindly. Or at least, she didn't *think* it was unkind. It was difficult to tell one way or another from twenty yards away.

"Move your ass, Han!" one of his friends shouted. They had made it to the edge of the parking lot and seemed to have only just realized Wire Glasses wasn't with them. "I'm hungry!"

"What else is new?" Wire Glasses shouted back, before turning again to Annette. "Are you sure you don't need a hand?"

"Don't worry about me," Annette said, trying to shoo him along. This whole thing was ridiculous, and she'd feel awful if she was the reason a stranger didn't eat lunch. Whether or not his frowns were meant kindly. "I just need a quick break and I'll be right as rain. Go along with your friends."

Wire Glasses stepped off the last stair, but although his body was facing his friends, his narrowed eyes were focused on Annette. *Really* focused. Like he was sizing her up in a poker game. Though god knew why that required such intensity. Annette had never been good at bluffing.

"Henry, come on," one of the women in the group called. "Mario's won't keep our reservation for more than five minutes."

Wire Glasses—Henry—stopped looking at Annette at last. She thought he would finally give up and walk off, leaving her alone to drag herself and her crumbling pride to the lodge at her own pace. Instead—"Go on without me," he told his friends. "I'll catch up."

"Henry," the woman called, sounding slightly affronted. "It's *Mario's*!"

But he'd already turned to trudge up the path toward Annette, and he didn't look back.

"I'm fine, really," Annette insisted, trying to get some traction in the snow with her ski poles so she could push herself up and prove her legs weren't as shaky as they felt. "You don't want to miss your reservation. Mario's is supposed to be the best Italian joint in Vermont. I can manage. Honestly. Look," she added through her teeth, forcing her burning muscles to support her weight. "See?" she ground out. "Fine."

"Ah, yes, of course," Henry said, nudging his glasses up his nose with the back of his glove. "I couldn't tell from back there, but that face you're making is clearly the grimace of a woman who is completely fine."

He said it without a single hint of humor in his expression, but Annette let out a bark of laughter before she even considered it might not have been meant as a joke.

He blinked at her, startled, and she dropped on her butt in the snowdrift, her stubbornness no match for her noodle legs.

"Sorry," she said with a rueful smile, massaging her calf with both hands. It was starting to cramp, the bastard. "My sense of humor can be obnoxious at times."

Henry frowned again. "Who told you that?"

"Don't tell me you weren't thinking it," Annette teased.

"I wasn't." He walked past her and plucked her skis out of the snow.

"Oh, come on. Serious guy like you? I doubt you're used to being cackled at by crazy snow hags."

"Not really," he admitted. "But that doesn't mean I dislike the experience." Inexplicably, Henry dropped down in the snowdrift beside her, leaning her skis against his shoulder. "If you must know, the only thing I was thinking was that it was nice to not have to explain I was joking for once."

Annette narrowed her eyes at him, hands still against her ankle, words temporarily deserting her.

"What?" he asked, the glint of humor she thought she'd spotted in his eyes slipping back behind a guarded frown.

"You're not going to insist on fetching the nearest medic to drag me the rest of the way to the lodge?"

He shrugged, his expression relaxing. "You said you were fine. I assumed that meant you were enjoying the scenery. I can't blame you, either." He pointed at the rows of sparkling cars partially hidden by snow-covered hedges beyond which his friends had disappeared. "The parking lot is enchanting from this angle."

So that *was* a dry sense of humor she'd detected. Fascinating. She gestured with her chin back the way she'd come. "And if you turn your head that way, you'll see the backs of some vending machines peeking out from the trees."

"Stunning," Henry said, following her gaze. "I can almost hear the buzz of the hot chocolate machine."

Annette let out a wistful sigh, wishing she had a hot chocolate right now to hold in her slowly freezing hands. And another in a hot water bottle to hold against the cramp in her leg. She winced as the cramp got worse, and stretched her leg out in front of her with a hiss.

Henry had locked his gaze on her again, his brow pinched, but he didn't try to override Annette's insistence that she didn't need help. And maybe that was why she didn't feel like she'd be losing face if she admitted she wasn't doing so hot.

"It's a cramp," she admitted through her teeth. "I pushed myself too hard with the skiing and they pulled me off the slope early. I thought I could manage to walk back—it's not that far to the lifts—but my legs have lost their bones and—" She gasped, tears springing to her eyes as pain seared through her calf. "Holy hell, this cramp is vindictive."

"What do you need?" Henry asked.

"I don't know. A Saint Bernard?"

"Good thinking." Henry nodded as though she'd suggested something very wise. "A Saint Bernard would be exactly the thing. Though I'm not sure where to find any. I'd have to ask around. Might be quicker if I took you back to the lodge myself."

The lodge. Hot apple cider and warmth and comfortable couches. And food. Boy, was she hungry. Her stomach rumbled and she patted it, promising it calories soon.

"How do you propose to get me there, though?" she asked. "I'm not sure I can hobble all the way, even with you on one side and one of these"—she lifted a hand and let the ski pole attached to her wrist dangle—"on the other. They make for terrible crutches."

Henry stood and offered her a gloved hand. "Think you can manage to hop on my back?"

Annette eyed his glove, uncomfortably aware that there were still tears of pain clumping her eyelashes together. It was the kind of thing that would happen in a romantic comedy—where the heroine could spend the whole movie going from disaster to disaster and still end up falling right into the handsome hero's arms. But it wasn't something that happened in real life. Or if it did, it didn't happen to Annette. She was too small, too stubborn, too silly. If she was in a rom-com, she wouldn't get higher in the pecking order than "goofy best friend."

"What's the matter?" Henry asked, lifting his eyebrows.

"Well," Annette began nervously, "isn't that kind of . . . I mean, don't you think it would be awkward? You seem nice and all, but I hardly know you."

"Henry Han," he said, leaving his offered hand stretched between them. "Twenty-four. Born and raised in New York. Two sisters, no brothers."

"Pets?"

He didn't quite smile, but she could tell he wanted to. "My grandmother had a cat when I was little. A gray tabby named Jingyi. He hated anyone who wasn't my grandmother."

Huffing a laugh through the pain, Annette put her glove in his. "Annette Lim. Twenty-three. Born in San Diego, raised in Connecticut. No siblings. I had a goldfish named Silver when I was eight. And I have to be honest with you about something: I'm not a snow hag."

A flicker of humor crossed his face, resolving into a kind of formal solemnity. "It's a pleasure to meet you, Annette Lim." His fingers were surprisingly firm and real as they shook hands, despite the thick layers of material between their skin. She could almost feel the warmth of his hand against her palm, though obviously that was impossible. "Do you want a lift, or should I go back for the Saint Bernard?"

Annette's grip tightened on his hand involuntarily, not wanting to be left alone in this snowdrift when she was cold and frustrated and in pain. "I'm . . . I'm actually allergic to dogs," she said. "So as long as you don't mind . . . ?"

"Not at all. I'm headed your way, after all. Better for the environment if we go together, right?"

Annette snorted and let him help her to her feet. Within a few seconds she was settled on his back, her skis in one hand, Henry's elbows folded securely around the backs of her knees. She might have been more concerned about the prospect of wrapping herself around a strange man, but Henry didn't have a hint of that gross calculating look of a man with ulterior motives. Besides, her coat had so much padding it probably felt like carting around the Michelin Man.

The movement was nice, too. Henry had a good walk. Steady. Like a rocking chair. The kind you could settle into on a big front porch to watch fireflies in the twilight. She sighed, closing her eyes as pain worked its way further into her body. The cramp seemed to be moving from her calf straight to her head.

"Tell me if you need to get down or anything," Henry said.

"Okay." Pain seared up her leg, bringing a sweaty rush of nausea with it, and she pressed her face against the collar of his coat, dragging in a lungful of air through her nose. The glare of the sun was blocked out at once, and she was enveloped in a pleasant scent—a sort of woodsy, smoky aroma combined with something vaguely sweet, like the smell of sweet potatoes roasting.

"Still with me, Annette?"

"Mmm-hmm," she murmured, not daring to move. She liked the way he said her name. He didn't try to christen her with a nickname first thing like a lot of people did, reducing her name to "Annie" or—even worse—"Netty," like she was a child. Or a pet. And he smelled really nice. Since when did guys smell this nice?

Her leg seized and she bit back a whimper, tensing up all over.

"Annette?"

"It's just the cramp," she said, her voice muffled by his coat.

"I can walk slower."

"I like how you're walking. But—Actually, do you know what might help? Could you talk about something? It hurts less when I have something else to concentrate on."

"What do you want me to talk about?"

"I don't know. Doesn't matter. Tell me about your friends. How long have you known each other?"

Annette's pink marshmallow ski coat didn't provide enough padding to stop her from noticing the substantial whoosh of air leaving Henry's lungs. "Too long, probably," he said.

"Why? What's wrong with them?"

"No, they're fine. Just . . . overly meddlesome. I won't be so put out once I'm off this damn mountain."

As much as Annette wanted to ask him what they'd done that was so meddlesome, she got the feeling he'd already gone into as much detail as he was willing to share. Lifting her face, she instead rested her chin on his shoulder, eyes closed against the sun reflecting off ice and snow. The nausea seemed to have passed as quickly as it came, thank goodness. She would've been mortified if she'd ended up barfing all over this nice boy's coat. "Are you not big on the flinging-yourself-down-a-mountain thing, then?"

His shoulder relaxed a fraction of an inch under her chin. "Not really. It's more of a height thing than a flinging thing, though. I'm not a fan of high places."

"Good thing you decided to vacation on top of a mountain."

He turned his head toward her for a moment, but her eyes were still closed against a budding headache and she didn't catch his expression. "I thought it would be ideal, yes. Watch your skis, we've got stairs."

3

The ceilings were lower around the ski entrance where they came in, though the decor was just as quaintly rustic as the rest of the lodge. The main difference was the back entrance had more of a busy bed-and-breakfast energy than the lush lobby in the front. No one was really hanging around the sitting area at the moment—people were mainly heading to the slopes or grabbing an early lunch from the small restaurant on the other side of the narrow staircase dividing the room—so Henry didn't have any trouble snagging the couch closest to the small fireplace.

"Thanks," Annette said when he'd set her down. She couldn't quite suppress a wince as she dragged one leg up to wrestle off her boot. "I'm sorry I kept you so long. Do you think you can still catch up to your friends?"

"They'll be okay without me for an hour or two," Henry said, loosening his scarf as he looked around the lobby. "Are your friends around?"

"They're still out skiing, but we were supposed to meet here for lunch. They'll show up soon."

"I don't get why they left you to walk back on your own," Henry said, another frown pinching his brow as the scarf came off, knocking his glasses a little crooked. Annette felt her index finger twitch, as though her hand wanted to reach up and set them right again. She quashed the impulse quickly. Just because he was happy to give her a lift didn't mean it was okay for her to fuss over his glasses for him.

Straightening his glasses with an automatic movement of his free hand, Henry sat on the edge of an ottoman and began absently folding his scarf. "Didn't they notice you left?"

"Maybe I was the only one on the bunny slopes," Annette said, lowering her gaze to her calf. It felt a little better with the warmth of the fire seeping through her clothes, and she thought massaging the muscle in here was doing more good than it had outside.

"Were you?"

"Well . . ." She was going to explain that she hadn't wanted to ruin the fun for anybody else just because she was stupid about how much she exerted herself, but that wasn't the whole truth. She took a deep breath and lifted her eyes to meet Henry's and blurted out, "I'm just so *sick* of it. Just because I'm short and I laugh a lot and I like the color pink doesn't mean I'm their mutant home ec flour-baby assignment. I don't expect you to believe this, since you just had to pull me out of a snowbank, but I'm usually extremely capable of taking care of myself. And I'm tired of everyone insinuating that I'm somehow in need of constant babysitting because I'm prioritizing grad school over planning a stupid wedding."

"Ah," Henry said. "So your friends are insufferable meddlers, too."

"Insufferable. Yes. That's a good word." She sighed, pressing her thumb into a particularly tight spot in the back of her calf.

"I'll be right back," Henry said, getting to his feet. He dropped his scarf and gloves on the ottoman and pointed at her, frowning. "Don't move. Seriously."

"I couldn't if I wanted to," Annette said, pointing back at him, mirroring his serious expression.

Henry nodded, appeased, and Annette smiled as she watched him stride toward the snack bar along the back wall. She wasn't quite sure what to make of him. If she had thought to categorize him before he pulled her out of the snow, she would have thought he'd be the brooding, quiet type—not shy, necessarily, just not really suited to crowded ski lodges on one of the busiest weekends of the season. Both times they'd crossed paths, he'd been a little removed from his circle of friends, his expression devoid of even the smallest hint of humor.

But maybe she had just glimpsed him at bad moments, because since he'd stopped to help he'd been . . . well, *funny*. And not in that competitive, almost desperate way Annette had come to resent in her dates. He hadn't precisely laughed at anything she'd said, but she found it didn't bother her like she would have expected. It wasn't as though he didn't acknowledge her jokes—he just did so by keeping the joke rolling. And by the subtle glint of appreciation in his eyes . . .

A second cramp redirected Annette's thoughts to her immediate problem. Grimacing, she yanked off her ski goggles and beanie and lay back on the couch, trying to breathe her way through the pain.

"The woman at the bar says they can bring in a medic from the first aid station if you need one." Henry's voice was a welcome distraction, and Annette opened her eyes to see him setting a tray on the side table above her head.

"I'm not injured," Annette ground out, pushing herself back into a sitting position. "Just stupid."

That made him frown that strangely caring frown of his. "You're not stupid, you've got muscle cramps. It happens. Here." He plucked something from the tray and held it out for Annette to take. "I brought some things to help."

A hot water bottle. Had she mentioned she wanted one? She didn't think so. "Henry Han," she said solemnly, sliding the perfectly warmed bottle under her leg, "you are hereby pronounced my favorite person on this mountain."

"I'm honored," Henry said, matching her tone and passing her a large regular water bottle with the resort's logo printed on the side. "Hydrating is supposed to help, too. *And*"—he ripped open a small paper pouch and laid two orange pills on her palm—"I even tracked down some Advil."

An intense wave of affection rushed through her chest, rendering her temporarily speechless. She lifted her gaze from the Advil in her palm to Henry's face. "I think I might have to marry you."

Henry sputtered out a breath. "I usually only accept appreciation in the form of thank-yous," he said, taking off his glasses to clean them on the edge of his shirt.

Annette bit her lips together to stop herself from wondering out loud if that meant he was willing to make an exception in her case. She was being silly—she'd had similar rushes of affection for the most average spaghetti in the world after a tiring day of hiking.

Yeah, the food, *Annette. Not the chef.*

She ignored that little observation and washed the Advil down with three big gulps of water. She was loopy from pain and overexertion and she'd gotten herself too wound up about the *you can't possibly be happy unless you're power-walking to the alter* lectures she kept getting. That was all. She didn't have any more feelings for Henry than she'd have for a plate of spaghetti. A really handsome, funny plate of spaghetti.

"One last question." Henry slid his glasses back on and pointed to the tray, where there remained two steaming mugs. "Hot chocolate or apple cider?"

Though she couldn't say she'd met a plate of spaghetti who'd been so heart-swellingly thoughtful. "I'll take the cider, if that's okay. Thank you," she added, finding his eyes so he knew she meant it. "Not many people would sacrifice a reservation at Mario's to help a difficult stranger."

"You're not difficult." He left the cider on the tray next to her and took the hot chocolate with him to the ottoman. "You're . . ." He searched her face as though the word he wanted was hiding just behind her eyes, or written around the edges of her mouth.

And it turned out she was wrong. How she felt wasn't about appeasing her friends and family. It wasn't a result of cramps. It sure as hell didn't have anything to do with spaghetti. She wanted him to stay right there and talk to her for hours. She wanted to cozy up beside him with her head on his shoulder, memorizing the warm, sweet, woodsy scent of him. She wanted to slip into his arms and steal a kiss, steal a dozen kisses. She wanted more of his kind grumpiness. More of his dry humor. More of *him*. And she wasn't entirely sure she could limit that want to one weekend.

There may have been more truth in her proposal than she'd realized.

"Henry," she began in a whisper, not entirely sure what she wanted to say—

The back doors banged open, and a large group of skiers bustled inside, talking and laughing and generally destroying any sense of intimacy the nearly-deserted sitting area had provided up until that point. Annette spotted Tracy's neon-green skis bobbing through the throng and cursed inwardly.

"Looks like at least one of my friends has returned from skiing," Annette said, her eyebrows pinching. She turned back to Henry, who had straightened, pulling away from her. Oh no. He was going to leave. *Do something.* "Do you want—"

"There you are!" Tracy shouted, making a beeline toward the fire, Paul in her wake.

Annette shot her a quick look which she hoped Tracy would realize meant she and Paul should take a detour to stow their ski things before charging the rest of the way over, but it was already too late.

"I should go," Henry was saying in a low voice, getting to his feet, his eyes fixed on his untouched mug of cocoa as he set it back on the tray. "Try not to get yourself stranded in any more snowbanks, okay?"

No, no, no. He couldn't leave. Not yet. She grabbed Henry's sleeve before he could escape. "Hey, wait. Stay. You can come with us to lunch. I'll buy. It's the least I can do since I made you miss out on Mario's."

"That's okay," he said, laying his hand over her fingers on his elbow and meeting her eyes. "I'm sure you're in good hands. Maybe I'll see you around later."

"Sure," Annette said, reluctantly releasing him. If he wanted to get away from her now that his Good Samaritan deed was done for the day, she wasn't going to change his mind by being clingy. "I'll—I'll keep an eye out for you?"

He hesitated one moment longer, his expression inscrutable. "Okay." He turned sharply and started a little when he discovered Tracy and Paul standing two armchairs away, staring at their exchange with excessive interest. "Excuse me," he muttered, striding around them.

Annette glared at her interfering friends. "Great timing, guys."

"Who was that?" Tracy asked, flinging herself on the couch next to Annette. "He seemed nice."

"Yeah." Annette spotted the flash of a red scarf by the stairs and watched as Henry started up them, scrubbing a hand through his gravity-defying black hair. "He is."

4

Annette got up bright and early the next day with the same breathless anticipation that used to come with childhood Christmas mornings. Only she couldn't remember Christmas ever inspiring the nervous little knot which tugged at her stomach as she spread outfit options on the bed. Or the tremble in her fingers as she applied her makeup.

She had only seen Henry once more yesterday, and only in passing. Annette's friends had been herding her out the door for a dinner reservation at a steak house in town, and Henry was standing with two of his friends, hands in his pockets, looking mutinous. She'd managed to catch his eye and offer a wave and a smile, since that was about all she could do without breaking out of the center of the chattering stampede of her own friends. She imagined his shoulders relaxed a fraction, and his expression, at least for a moment, didn't seem so tense as he lifted a hand in a small wave of his own. But the moment had been fleeting, and had left her feeling anxious.

She just didn't have a lot of time. There was no way any of the lodge's guests this weekend hadn't planned to stay for the Valentine's Day shindig later tonight. There would be a big, swanky party downstairs and the fireworks display the lodge did every year was supposed to rival their New Year's spectacle. But that meant she only had maybe twenty-four hours to figure out whether there was any substance to her acute case of attraction. And if she ever wanted to see Henry again after they got off this mountain, she at *least* needed to get his phone number. Ideally without any of his meddlesome friends getting in the way.

Annette was humming another song—Cher, this time—as she hurried down the main staircase in her pale pink sweater and wool skirt, coat over her arm, scanning the quiet lobby for any sign of Henry or his red scarf.

She paused halfway down the stairs and leaned over the banister, trying to get a better view of the sitting area around the fire. Henry was nowhere to be seen. She didn't recognize any of his friends, either. Only a few people were hanging around the fire at this hour—early risers with their cups of joe and their breakfast pastries and their morning newspapers.

Annette's shoulders drooped. She'd had some silly Disney idea in the back of her mind that she'd glide elegantly down the lavish staircase with Henry looking up at her like the world had come to a standstill. And as silly as she knew it was, she was disappointed that it wouldn't come true.

The Doc Martins were probably not her best choice if she had really wanted to *glide*, she thought ruefully, clomping down another few steps. And 7:18 a.m. was frankly a ridiculous time to expect anyone to be standing at the bottom of a staircase waiting to be awed by a dork in a pink sweater.

A tap on her elbow made her jump and whip her head around. Henry had appeared beside her on the staircase, his approach rendered silent by the thunk of her shoes. His glasses seemed to glint with an extra sparkle in the early morning sun streaming through the picture windows.

"You're up early," he said. The tiniest flicker of a smile touched his lips, like lightning on the horizon. Too distant to ever expect to catch, but bright and electric. Annette felt it crackle through her, making the hairs on her arms and the back of her neck stand on end.

"Hi!" she said, beaming at him. Her hand had attached itself to his arm when she wasn't paying attention, but she refused to take it back. She was the opposite of coy and she didn't care. She didn't have time for coy. "Listen, where are your friends?"

Henry looked only mildly surprised, bless him. Anyone else would have been downright alarmed at her exuberance. "Still sleeping, probably. Why?"

"Mine too. Want to come with me into town?"

"What?"

"You said you hate skiing, and I think I do too, after yesterday, so do you want to ditch the meddling posse and play tourist in town?"

"Just you and me?"

"Yeah. Is that okay?"

He touched his glasses, though they didn't appear to need adjusting, as his eyes flicked to the top of the stairs. "I . . . Okay."

Annette only barely stopped herself from flinging both arms around him and squeezing with all her might. "Really?"

"Yeah," he said with a stubborn kind of frown. "That actually sounds great."

"Great," Annette said, grabbing his hand and pulling him down the stairs. "Let's go."

"Wait, wait," Henry protested when they hit the ground floor. "Shouldn't we leave notes at the front desk or something?"

Annette stopped, wanting to tell him it wasn't necessary. But Tracy was likely to call in a search-and-rescue if she lost track of anyone in the party for more than half an hour. Annette didn't actually want to *worry* anyone.

"Fine," she relented, making a sharp right, her hand still firmly gripping Henry's. "Quickly, though."

"Of course, quickly," Henry said, giving her fingers the ghost of a squeeze. The knot in her stomach transformed into a flock of fluttering, hopeful sparrows.

Annette's note was short and to the point: *Don't flip out, I went into town for breakfast. With a boy. No chaperones, please!* She folded it over and passed it to the clerk and picked up a map while Henry finished scribbling his own note. She was pretty sure she could find the town without help, but she'd been in the back seat of Tracy's Range Rover when they drove up for dinner yesterday, and it had been dark. It didn't hurt to have a map to consult.

"Ready?" she asked, turning to Henry as she pulled her coat on.

"Ready." He shoved the pen and paper across to the clerk. "Let's go," he said, grabbing her hand and tugging her, laughing, into the clear, cold air outside.

"Okay, I know you don't like heights," Annette said as she pumped up the heat in the station wagon, hoping to quickly get rid of the fog and any ice her scraper had missed before they pulled out of the parking lot. "And I don't like driving in the snow—"

"So we're the ideal pair to be driving around an icy mountain," Henry said, tugging his seatbelt snug. "Perfect."

Annette snorted. "I just mean that I don't know about you, but I do better when I'm distracted. And since my radio is busted, you may find yourself bombarded with really stupid jokes. You don't have to laugh, but I'd appreciate it if you occasionally tell me how witty I am."

"I think I can do that."

"Cool." She checked her mirrors and patted her coat to make sure she had her wallet and the tube of pink lipstick she felt a little ridiculous for bringing with her on a semi-impromptu not-technically-a-date. She was very aware that Henry was watching her from his side of the car, but suddenly she couldn't quite bring herself to look at him. She felt like she might explode into a million colorful sparks if she caught him looking at her with that thoughtful intensity in such close quarters, and she still had an icy mountain road to drive.

Know what? Forget the tiny patch of fog left on the windshield. She could see just fine.

"Last chance to change your mind," she warned, twisting around and reversing out of her parking spot.

"Oh shit," Henry said, dropping in his seat like he was being shot at in an action movie.

"What?" Annette asked, hitting the brakes and scanning the area for snipers. "What's the matter?"

"Just get us out of here," Henry said, pulling his scarf up over his face. "Quick."

"Okay," Annette said, shifting into drive and pulling out of the parking lot with nothing more dramatic than the soft hiss of tires across slushy pavement. "But just so you know, I'm not sure I could outrun the law in this thing, even without the ice problem."

"What?"

Annette risked a glance at him as she turned onto the bumpy, wooded road that twisted down to the highway. He was still scrunched in his seat, though he'd dropped the scarf from over his nose. He was looking at her like she'd spoken to him in Klingon.

"What's with the duck-and-cover routine?" she asked.

"Ah." He peeked nervously over his shoulder as he sat up straight. "Nothing. I'm just . . . *really* tired of getting ambushed."

"Let me guess," Annette said. "The meddlers."

"*Insufferable* meddlers," Henry corrected darkly.

"What did they do? I mean, my friends are getting on my nerves, but I'm a long way from diving under the dashboard to avoid them."

"Yes, but I'm guessing your friends have *some* respect for normal human boundaries. Mine are more into . . . deciding how I should deal with things and then harassing me until I do what they want." He sagged against the window, face turned away from her. "Sorry. You were supposed to be bombarding me with witty jokes. You don't want to listen to me complain."

"The jokes will keep. Gossip is almost as good for distraction as jokes, anyway. Maybe better—my sense of humor always gets mega-cringey when I'm nervous."

"I don't mind cringey."

"Tell your auntie Annette what's troubling you," she said, patting his arm as the station wagon rumbled slowly between the trees. "I'll even promise not to tell you how to feel about it."

Henry shook his head. "Thanks, but I don't want to ruin the fun. I'll snap out of it."

Annette wasn't sure about that. It wasn't the first time he'd mentioned having an issue with his friends, she'd yet to see him look like he was enjoying their company at all, and even thinking about them seemed to make him fume. If those weren't signs that he needed to get something off his chest, she didn't know what was.

"Okay, I'll guess," she decided. "They want you to join their obsessive Captain Jean-Luc Picard fan club."

He snorted. "What?"

"No? Then they're pressuring you to take up snorkeling."

"I wish."

Rolling to a stop at the end of the lodge's entrance road, Annette sat forward to check she was one hundred percent clear to make a cautious left turn. The town was a little way further up the highway, right before the last climb to the pass. "No, wait, I got it: they're all very disappointed that your dislike of heights means you have yet to realize your potential as a high-wire circus performer."

"Close. They want me to get back together with my ex."

Annette's foot slipped on the gas pedal and the station wagon pulled out onto the highway with a crunch. Whatever she'd been expecting the problem to be, it wasn't that. "What?"

"Yeah. In fact, so convinced were they that this was the right thing to do, they managed to sneak her up here and spring her on me right after we checked in."

"Oh." Annette kept her eyes fixed determinedly on the highway, feeling silly for thinking he'd come with her because he had also felt a draw between them. All he'd wanted was to get some peace from his friends. He'd said as much yesterday, too, after he dragged her out of the snowbank. He would have probably agreed to an excursion with an eighty-year-old, tobacco-chewing biker carrying a sawn-off shotgun if it meant a few hours without them.

"I don't know why they thought it would be a good idea," Henry went on, warming to the rant. "We broke up over a year ago and I think we've talked all of two times since. We just weren't going in the same direction, and we argued about everything. I thought we were at least on the same page about splitting up. But apparently not, since from what I can gather, she's been telling all our friends it was a mistake and she wants to get back together." He pushed his glasses up to rub his eyes. "I guess no one thought it was worth getting my opinion on the matter."

Annette risked a sideways glance at his profile, but she was having a hard time interpreting his stormy expression. "What *is* your opinion on the matter?"

"It wasn't a mistake," Henry said firmly. "We were never a good team, and I'm not . . . we're not in love anymore. Even if I hadn't been sure about splitting up before, this whole ambush situation would've convinced me I did the right thing. I swear, if I hadn't carpooled up here with a bunch of assholes, I would've gone straight back home on Friday."

Annette bit her lip as she steered around a wide curve in the highway, debating how to respond. She didn't blame him for not wanting to stick around after his ex turned up. Annette certainly wouldn't have stayed, if Tracy had decided to fix her "spinster problem" by shoving one of Paul's residency buddies at her without warning. But she didn't like the reality Henry leaving would have created—a reality in which they missed each other by minutes. It seemed so terribly melancholy. But she couldn't tell him that. She'd sound insane—even more so than after her painkiller-inspired proposal yesterday—and there was no way she could sell it as a joke.

Navigating this conversation was turning out to be more nerve-wracking than navigating the icy highway.

"Is it insensitive of me to say I'm glad you stuck around?" she ventured. "And not just because you saved me from hypothermia yesterday in the nicest, sweetest, least asshole-ish way possible?"

She could feel his eyes on her, but she didn't dare

check his expression, too afraid of what she'd find written in subtle strokes across his face.

"Be honest," he said at last. "The Saint Bernard would have been better company."

Annette shook her head, smiling as the tension lifted. "You're definitely a better conversationalist. Plus, you don't make me sneeze."

"And that makes up for me being such a grump?"

"There's nothing to make up for," Annette said. "You're a friendly grump. I like to have a friendly grump or two in my life. Keeps things interesting."

"In that case," Henry said slowly, "maybe I'm glad I stuck around, too. And not just because you saved me from being ambushed this morning in the funnest, kindest, most frightening way possible."

Annette huffed out a laugh, unconvinced he was referring only to the sharp drop beyond the guard rail. Because she was pretty scared herself. A good kind of scared, though. The kind of scared she'd been when she'd moved away to college. The kind of scared that meant she was heading toward something big and life-altering and *good*. Not that it required any less bravery.

"Annette?"

"Yeah?"

"I don't think I've mentioned yet how witty you are."

Annette slapped his shoulder lightly with the back of her hand. "You're supposed to wait until I make a stupid joke to tell me that, Henry."

"Well, it's true," he said. "And if I waited until one of your jokes was stupid, I think I'd be waiting forever." He'd twisted away from the window slightly and now let his temple fall against the headrest, watching her with an intensity she could feel even without looking over.

She'd give him one thing: he was extremely distracting. "What?"

"Nothing. I'm just . . . happy I ran into you."

5

The town was nestled into a gentle, evergreen-mantled valley. It was charmingly idyllic with its quaint shops and bistros and bakeries that looked, to Annette, like rows of life-sized gingerbread houses. The first thing they did was stop for breakfast at a place on Main Street that was supposed to have excellent pancakes. Despite the early hour, the little bistro was crowded with rowdy skiers preparing for a day on the slopes, plus a handful of quieter townies at the counter.

Annette and Henry ended up at the counter too, after agreeing they were too hungry to wait forty minutes for a table. Though Annette couldn't judge whether the pancakes lived up to the hype—she was too absorbed in her conversation with Henry to spare much attention for her taste buds. They weren't even talking about anything particularly groundbreaking. Most of the topics were the standard first-date litany—favorites in music, TV, books, everything else; brief bios of any and all living relatives; where they went to school and what they majored in and what they planned to do in the future—but it didn't feel like playing awkward small talk bingo. It was fascinating and important and every anecdote, every question, made Annette more certain that a few hours with Henry weren't going to be enough.

After a brief squabble over who would pay the bill—which Henry eventually won by way of insisting he owed her for kidnapping him away from the lodge—they wandered back outside where the rest of the town was slowly coming to life.

"What do you want to do next?" Annette asked, squeezing the gold-and-black cylinder of lipstick in her coat pocket like a talisman.

Henry glanced around the shop windows, half of which still proclaimed themselves "closed." Their options at the moment—at least those in the immediate vicinity—were another restaurant, a kitschy souvenir shop with an excess of tinsel showering the window display, a compact little consignment store, and a cozy bakery with shelves and shelves of pastries crammed into the large window.

"Do you feel like taking a walk?" he asked, touching the bridge of his glasses and not quite meeting her eyes. Like he was nervous. About asking her to take a walk.

It was so adorable Annette just about flung her arms around him again.

She caught herself in time, but she couldn't help the too-wide grin on her face. "I could take a walk."

"You'll say something if you need to take a break, though," Henry said, peering at her seriously. "Won't you?"

"I won't need to take a break," Annette said, flipping an airy hand. The sidewalks were clear of snow, and it wasn't even that hilly in town. "As long as I don't try skiing down the rooftops, I doubt the cramps will come back."

"But if you need to stop for a minute—"

"I'll squeeze your hand," Annette said boldly, stretching out her bare fingers—she hadn't yet pulled on her gloves after leaving the restaurant. She realized a moment later that she should probably not be quite *that* bold with a man who had been navigating a tricky ex situation all weekend and added, "If that's okay, I mean."

Henry's frown eased from his features as he reached out and slowly, gently took her hand. Not like he was unsure, or even like he was scared of breaking her, but like it was an important moment and he wanted to do it right. His fingers brushed across her palm and—

Oh. They'd clasped hands before, but not like this. He wasn't helping her out of a snowbank. She wasn't dragging him down a staircase as they made a silly break for freedom. This was deliberate, heart-pounding, skin-on-skin contact. Annette could feel every point where Henry's hand touched hers, sending shivers of awareness straight to her core. It took somewhere between an eternity and no time at all for their palms to settle against each other, hands linked perfectly.

"Let's go," Henry said softly, starting down the sidewalk at a stroll, still watching her face.

"Okay," Annette replied, her voice pitched strangely high.

There was that lightning flicker of a smile again, crackling the air around them with electricity. Annette swallowed, trying to remember why it was a bad idea to chase after that lightning smile with her mouth. To slide her free hand through his short, black hair as she pulled him close.

She made herself look away and spotted a little bookstore on the corner across the street. "Ooh, we should stop in there when they open," she said, pointing. "Though—I probably shouldn't, actually. I already have more books with me than I can read."

He shrugged. "So? I'm not sure it counts as a vacation unless you come home with more books than you brought with you."

"Enabler."

Henry squeezed her hand and they circled back around to their discussion of books. Annette even admitted to owning four different editions of *Pride and Prejudice*—something she normally wouldn't have mentioned until she'd known someone a little longer for fear they'd think her crazy. But it turned out Henry had multiple copies of The Shining, two of which were identical except that one was kept neatly on the shelf while the other was dog-eared and written in, with a spine which had been taped back together more than once.

They stopped in a small square a few blocks from the bistro, settling on a bench in the wide, empty gazebo in the center of the snow-covered lawn, their hands still clasped.

"What are you thinking about?" Henry asked.

She looked over at him. "Hmm?"

"You're frowning."

"Oh." She hadn't noticed, but he was right. She offered a reassuring smile. "Nothing bad. I just . . . Can I ask you something personal? You don't have to answer if you don't want to."

Henry looked wary, but he nodded. "Sure."

"Maybe it's just because I don't know your friends, but from what you've told me they sound kind of . . . horrible? And you're obviously not. So why not hang out with less-horrible people?"

Henry drew in a slow, exhausted-sounding breath and scrubbed a hand through his hair. "It's . . . complicated."

"Okay," Annette said, watching his profile closely. She would have reminded him again that he didn't have to answer, but she thought his expression indicated that he was wrestling with what to say, not so much that he was trying to get out of answering at all. So she waited.

"I'm not . . . I'm not what you'd call a people person," he said at last, focusing on their linked hands. "I was the kid in school who hid behind a book at lunch, who sat at the back of the classroom and dreaded being called on to answer questions. My family thought I was shy. I think my classmates and teachers thought I was sullen. Mostly I was just . . . lonely. And I couldn't figure out how not to be. No one wanted to talk to me for longer than a few minutes. At some point I just gave up trying to connect with anyone."

"Henry," Annette said. "That's so sad."

He looked at her, his expression softening. "It's okay. It didn't last forever. I met Keith in high school. You might have seen him around. He's the tall one with the crooked nose. He was the first person who actually *wanted* to hang out with me. He took me under his wing, so to speak, and I went from having nobody to talk to but my family to having a whole group of friends."

"Who you have described to me more than once as being assholes," Annette pointed out.

He shrugged. "I'm not going to say they don't drive me up the wall sometimes, or that they're particularly *good* friends, but . . . I mean, people like me, we don't always have too many options."

"What do you mean, 'people like you?'" Annette said, twisting on the bench to face him better. No one would have ever accused her of being shy, but she'd been slapped with the *silly* label often enough to know how much it sucked to have your entire, complex self reduced to one easily dismissed word. "People who are funny and nice?"

"People who aren't actually good at talking to other people."

"You're doing great with me."

"Only because you're easy to talk to." He reached out tentatively to straighten her coat collar between his fingers. "I don't know if you understand how weird and how . . . *miraculous* it is for me to hit it off with anyone as fast as . . . as this."

Annette couldn't help a small, embarrassed smile. "You think we're hitting it off?"

"Don't you?"

"Well, yeah. But I guess . . . I guess I wasn't sure if I was just being . . . silly. I mean, the only reason you came over yesterday was because I was on my butt, cry-laughing in the snow. I wouldn't call that a sparkling first impression."

"It wasn't the *only* reason," Henry said softly, watching her face with an intensity that made it hard to breathe. "It was also because when you walked in the lobby the night before I thought you were . . ."

"Obnoxious?" Annette offered in a kind of knee-jerk compulsion to break the intensity. To give her a little space to think.

He frowned, which only intensified his gaze. "No, Annette. I was going to say—"

"Silly?" she squeaked, her heart hammering in her throat.

His frown deepened. "Annette."

"Bombastic, maybe?" she tried desperately. They had to snap out of this. Didn't they? Surely there had been a good reason she'd stopped herself from throwing herself into his arms ten times already. If she could just remember what any of them were . . .

"Annette," he said, even softer, his bare fingers grazing her cheek.

A jolt went through her at his touch and she bit her lip, trying to mask the way her breath hitched. They'd gotten closer since she last took a normal breath. She didn't know if it was her who'd closed the gap or him, but there were only inches between them now, and the only things she was aware of were related directly to Henry—his hand in hers, his fingers barely touching the sensitive area under her ear, every striation of brown in his eyes, the odd way the air between them felt warmer than it should have been.

"You were like a ray of sun breaking through the clouds," he said, his frown turning worried, like he wasn't sure how she'd react. "You seemed full to bursting with joy and I just . . . I wanted to get closer to that. I wanted to talk to you so much. And that was before I realized how much I like just about everything about you."

"What a coincidence," Annette said breathlessly. She was overwhelmed by another warm, insistent rush of affection that made it hard to work out what she *wanted*. It felt so complicated and life-changing—all she knew was she wanted *more*. "I like you too. I like how sweet you are. I like how funny you are. I like how comfortable it is to talk to you. I can't actually think of anything about you I *don't* like."

Some of the worry cleared from his expression as the corner of his mouth twitched into a hesitant smile. "Annette," he said, reverent. As though her name was the most important word he'd ever uttered.

"Yes?" She curled one finger to trace the center of his palm and he let out a short burst of air in response, as though he was just as aware, just as distracted by her as she was by him. Somehow there was almost no space between them at all now. Her eyes fluttered shut as the tip of her nose brushed against Henry's.

"Please let me kiss you," he breathed.

Yes. That. She wanted that. Lifting her chin with the barest movement, she touched her lips against his with the same slow deliberation Henry had taken to accept her hand. Taking her time not because she was unsure, not because she was scared, but because this moment, right now, felt monumental. And by god, she was going to do it right.

Henry's fingers curled around her earlobe as he returned her kisses with careful, decadent precision. Every touch, every shared breath seemed to unlock all the things Annette hadn't dared to let herself want. She wanted *this*. She wanted to be more than the goofy sidekick, she wanted someone who could love her without any caveats, she wanted to fall in love without needing to assert again and again that her goals, her *dreams* weren't any less important or less crucial to her happiness than anyone else's.

She lifted the hand not entwined with Henry's and laid it flat against the soft cable sweater he was wearing under his coat, searching for the joint rhythms of his heart and his lungs. He didn't make her feel like what she wanted didn't matter. He didn't make her feel foolish for acting like herself. He thought she was clever, and he thought she was funny, and he thought she was kind.

Annette flicked her tongue along Henry's bottom lip, asking for more. He didn't hesitate to grant her wish, deepening their kisses with that same luxurious patience as before. Annette made a low sound in her throat and fisted her hand in his sweater, tugging him closer still. Maybe it was silly, maybe it didn't make any sense—they'd only met yesterday—but she *knew* she wanted this man in her life.

"Henry," she whispered between kisses. "I . . ." She thought it would be easy to ask, with the way he was kissing her and with what he'd just had the courage to tell her, but the question got stuck in her throat.

"What is it?" he asked, kissing her cheek, her nose. "What do you need?"

You, she thought, keeping her eyes tight shut against a strange press of . . . it felt like homesickness.

"Annette?" he asked, stroking his thumb across her cheekbone.

"I'm being silly," she said, trying to wave off her feelings. She made herself look at Henry and forced a smile. "This just doesn't happen to me. I don't get kissed in gazebos by sweet, attractive men who say they like just about everything about me. And I—I don't know where you're at with this, but I'm not sure I'm prepared to leave you behind when I go home."

Henry huffed out a breath, dropping a thoughtful gaze to their twined fingers. "No, I'm . . . I'm there too," he said slowly. "I want to keep seeing you after this, if you're okay with that. I just . . . I'm not sure it's a good idea to talk about it until I've got my meddler problem sorted out. They all still seem to think they can wear me down about this ex thing and I need to tell them once and for all that it's not going to happen. I need to tell Shannon it's not going to happen." He let out a heavy breath and rubbed his forehead with the heel of his free hand. "I'm sorry. I didn't mean to drag you into the middle of this. I should have just had it out with them yesterday. Hell, I should have said something after we checked in."

Annette squeezed his fingers. "You don't have to apologize," she said. "They're your friends, even if they act like assholes sometimes. And I don't—I don't want you to feel like you have to choose between being lonely again and going on another date with me."

"If the choice *they're* giving me is a choice between lonely and miserable it's not much of a choice, though." He raised his eyes to meet hers. "I'll sort it out when we get back. And then can we talk again tonight? You're staying for the party, aren't you?"

Annette managed an encouraging smile, though her stomach was in knots of anxiety. "I'll be there."

Henry pressed another long, gentle kiss to the corner of her mouth. "I'll find you," he promised in a murmur.

6

Annette spent most of the afternoon pretending she wasn't a ball of zapping nerves. She couldn't stand the idea of fretting herself to death in her room, so she'd tracked down a handful of her friends to make a trek to the second skier's lodge up near the bunny slopes, where she could fret herself to death at the arcade.

She had hoped she could stop herself from worrying about whether Henry would change his mind about everything he'd said this morning as he talked to his friends. The arcade was certainly raucous and flashy enough to drown out the thoughts of any remotely rational human being. But even with all the distractions, Annette couldn't seem to keep herself in the present.

It wasn't like she didn't trust him. She did. More than she probably should after about two days' worth of acquaintance. But she was also keenly aware that she had significantly less claim on Henry's time and affection than a group of people he'd known for years. If it came down to a choice between his friends and her, the logical choice, the right choice, would be his friends. Wouldn't it? Annette didn't think much of them, but she didn't actually *know* any of them. They were probably all perfectly nice people. Perfectly nice people who had every right to point out how irrational and silly it was to give up on getting back together with an old girlfriend in favor of dating someone he'd known for two days.

Annette couldn't even come up with a reasonable counterargument in her own head. Getting so attached to anyone that fast *was* irrational. It *was* silly. She'd been telling herself all weekend to slow down, to think more clearly. A futile effort, since it had taken her less than half an hour of conversation before she *proposed*. In jest, but still.

And yes, Henry said he wanted to keep seeing her. And yes, he said he liked just about everything about her. And yes, when he kissed her she felt brave and sure and radiant.

But that didn't mean they hadn't fallen into some joint delusion, imagining all the things they felt—everything they said—wouldn't crumble when faced with the reality of day-to-day life, with grad school and work and distance putting pressure on their untested affection.

"Hello? Earth to Annette."

She blinked out of her reverie and discovered Tracy giving her a look across the air hockey table. "What?"

"It's no fun finally being able to trounce you at this game when you're too spaced out to serve."

"Sorry." Irritated with herself, Annette focused on the table, discovered the puck sitting motionless four inches from her striker, and swiftly knocked it into the opposite goal before Tracy could react. The digital score board indicated they were now at 6–2 Tracy. "Better?"

"A little." Tracy threw the puck back on the table and lined up her shot. "Are you okay? You've been acting strange since you came back from breakfast."

Tracy's serve was quick but not precise, and Annette didn't have any trouble getting the puck under her control. "I'm fine," she said curtly, shooting it back.

"Did he turn out to be a jerk?" Tracy asked, fumbling her way out of conceding another point.

"No." Her stomach clenched at the memory of his voice as he promised to find her this evening. Which distracted her just long enough to allow Tracy to score the last goal.

"Good game," Annette said, flicking her striker toward the center of the table and turning for the veranda doors. It was getting too stuffy in here.

"Then what happened?" Tracy asked, following after her. "You've been swooning over this guy all weekend, and suddenly you're staring into space like the world is coming to an end—"

"I haven't been swooning over anybody," Annette snapped. It was a ridiculous claim, since she'd spent most of yesterday gushing about him whenever the opportunity presented itself while Tracy smirked at her knowingly. But she was too antsy to have this conversation in a hot, crowded arcade. The humid, chill air was a relief when she shoved out onto the peaceful veranda.

The sky seemed to stretch out forever overhead, the sharp colors of the afternoon giving way to dusky purples and warm yellows as the sun made its descent. The wide deck was suspended over bristling pine trees sweeping down into deeper and deeper shadow. Far down below, visible only from the very edge of the veranda, and mostly obscured by evergreens, was the lodge. Where Henry was. Where he'd promised to find her in a few hours.

Annette gripped the sturdy railing with her bare hands, trying not to think about how easy it would be for him to break her heart when he did.

Tracy stood beside her, leaning on her elbows, silently taking in the view. The others were still inside, and it was quiet in that corner of the veranda. The crowd of the afternoon had thinned significantly as dusk gathered and guests started heading down to get ready for the party.

"I'm ridiculous, aren't I," Annette said, her gaze stuck on the gentle twist of distant chimney smoke in the air above the lodge.

"I wouldn't say that," Tracy said.

Annette shook her head. "I am, though. I'm out here falling hard and fast for a guy I met on a weekend getaway and it doesn't make any sense."

"Why not?"

"It's too . . . perfect. He's so sweet, and I like him so much. And I can't quite figure out—It's—" She couldn't seem to find the words to explain her anxieties. "I'm not Elizabeth Bennet," she tried. "I'm Charlotte Lucas. I'm not supposed to get the handsome guy and the pretty speeches and the sweep-you-off-your-feet romantic gestures. I'm supposed to be the emotional support. The comic relief. I'm supposed to be happy to fade into the background, content with a mundane, unremarkable life once the story is done with me."

"You are *not* Charlotte Lucas," Tracy said, frowning. "And no one is asking you to be."

"But I'm not Elizabeth Bennet, either."

"No, you're Annette Lim: actual, living human being. You are funny and competent and smart and the last thing you deserve is settling for an unhappy, unremarkable life."

Annette turned back to the picturesque vista quickly fading into shadow. She was so full of wants, and they all seemed so impossible. She wanted remarkable. She wanted perfect. She wanted Henry. And she couldn't justify any of them, even to herself.

"I'm just scared if I let myself believe that—that I don't have to settle for sidekick—I'll just be setting myself up to get hurt," she confessed in barely more than a whisper.

"Well, yeah, you might be," Tracy said. "But how will you know whether you can have a remarkable life if you don't go after it with your whole heart?"

Annette sighed and propped her chin on her fists. "I tried that with skiing and ended up falling on my face about twenty times."

"All the more reason for this one to work out." Tracy leaned over to nudge Annette with her shoulder. "And even if it doesn't, you've got an emotional support character right here to pick you back up."

Annette managed a crooked smile, feeling a little braver despite herself. "Thanks, not-Charlotte."

Tracy linked her arm through Annette's with a warm smile of her own. "You bet, not-Lizzie."

Annette dragged her feet getting ready for the party, unable to completely repress her nerves about how things were going to go. She hadn't so much as caught a glimpse of Henry's red scarf across the room since this morning and she had started to harbor a cold knot of terror that she would walk down to the party only to discover he'd already left. And that last, uncertain kiss they'd shared by her car before they'd parted ways earlier was going to turn out to be the last time she'd ever see him, the last time she'd ever hear his voice, the last time she'd breathe in the sweet, woodsy scent of him.

"I don't know if I can do this," she kept telling Tracy, who was perched on Annette's bed wearing a pretty blue gown, swinging her bare feet as she watched Annette fuss over her makeup in the bathroom mirror.

"You can," Tracy insisted. She had told Paul to meet them at the party so she and Annette could get ready together, like a couple of teenagers preparing for homecoming. She seemed to be under the impression Annette would chicken out and stay in her room all night if Tracy wasn't around to hustle her along. "We're already dressed. It would be a shame not to let anyone else see how stunning we look, at least for a couple of minutes. We can always leave if it turns out not to be any fun."

"*You* are stunning," Annette muttered, furiously smearing a swatch of lipstick on her wrist. Too brown. She dropped it in her makeup bag and dug out two more options. "*I* am cute." She had curled her shoulder-length hair, pulling the top half back into a black velvet scrunchie except for two wisps left free to frame her face. She'd done her eye makeup a little brighter than usual, which may not have been the best choice if she was going for sophisticated, no matter how much she liked the almost neon shade of pink eyeshadow.

The chic little black dress kept her from looking like she was going bowling or something, but she would hardly call herself *stunning*.

"No," Tracy said. "You are stunning. Your Henry guy is going to be knocked down speechless when he sees you."

If he was there at all. "Stop it. You're making me more nervous and I don't want to mess up my lipstick." Annette swatched another selection on her wrist and immediately discarded that one too. The rosy neutral was fine, but it wasn't what she wanted. What she wanted, she realized, was probably still in her coat pocket. She swept out of the bathroom and retrieved her lucky pink lipstick, swatching it on her way back just to be sure.

"Luck, don't fail me now," she muttered. Taking a deep breath to calm her nerves, she glided the lipstick over her mouth with practiced ease and stood back to check the effect.

And . . . it worked. The color somehow brought everything together into a look that could easily be described as classy. She still wasn't sure about *stunning*, but she felt . . . pretty. Maybe even beautiful.

Worried the short burst of confidence would desert her at any moment, Annette washed the lipstick off her wrist, slapped the bathroom light off, and marched out to get her pocketbook and room key. "Let's just go," she said, slipping into her black heels and yanking the door open. "Before I lose my nerve."

The party was in full swing by the time they made it to the decked-out banquet room downstairs. There were refreshment tables against the walls, and staff holding trays of champagne and sparkling grape juice and canapés were weaving through the crowd. A live band had set up on a small stage at one end of the room, in front of a large dance floor. The entire far wall was made up of windows reflecting back the warm lights of the large banquet room. Couples and families were everywhere, talking and eating and dancing.

And she didn't see Henry—or a single one of his friends—anywhere.

Annette's confidence smashed into particles like a snowball hitting the trunk of an evergreen.

"I don't know if I can do this," she said, grabbing Tracy's elbow as they started into the crowd. She felt scattered and nervous and she didn't know what she'd do if Henry had left without even leaving behind a phone number at the front desk. "What if—"

The crowd created a narrow path and Annette's toe caught on a nonexistent flaw in the smooth parquet as she caught sight of Henry across the room. He was dressed in a smart black suit and his short black hair was looking a little wild, as though he'd been running his fingers through it. He seemed agitated, gesticulating sharply as he said something to one of his friends. Did that mean they were still arguing? Should she get out of the way? Or did Henry need backup? What was she supposed to do? She hadn't planned for this.

Before she could figure it out, the reedy guy Henry was talking to spotted her. He tapped Henry's arm and jerked his head in her direction.

Then Henry's eyes had found her. And he was looking at her like the whole world had come to a standstill. And maybe it had, because everything else seemed to fade into obscurity. The band, the crowd, even Tracy. For one breathless, suspended moment, there was only Annette standing there with her uncertain, hopeful heart and Henry across the room wearing an expression she was too frightened to claim she could interpret.

Henry started forward to meet her as though the crowd wasn't there, his eyes never leaving her face.

She couldn't move. She told herself he was only coming to tell her he made a mistake when he kissed her in the square this morning. She told herself he was only coming to apologize for leading her on—

He came to a stop an agonizing three or four steps away. She might have been fooling herself, but she thought she saw some of her own raw, overwhelming *want* echoed back to her in the intensity of his gaze.

"Hi," he said, touching his glasses nervously.

"Hi," she said in an oddly raspy voice.

"I was afraid you weren't coming."

She huffed out a thready sort of laugh. "I was afraid you'd left already."

"Not for anything," Henry said vehemently, moving toward her another step. "Annette, I wouldn't know how to walk away from you even if I wanted to. I haven't been able to get you out of my head since you tumbled into the lodge Friday afternoon, and I've liked you more every second I've known you. And I think . . . I know this is going to sound crazy, but I think . . . I think I'm falling in love with you."

She couldn't help the adoring smile on her face any more than she could help the irrational, glorious rush of affection swelling in her heart, crowding out all the *should*s and *never-gonna-happen*s. No one was stopping her from being the heroine of this story except herself. And that was crazier than anything else she'd thought all weekend.

"Annette?" he asked, his brow pinched with worry.

"Yes," she said at once. "Yes, yes, yes."

Henry seemed mildly alarmed. "Yes to—to what?"

"Everything." She felt as though she were gliding as she closed the last of the space he'd left between them. She rested her hands lightly on his shoulders, letting herself want everything, letting herself believe she deserved it. "You. Us. Being with you. Falling in love. Everything."

"Annette Lim," he muttered, brushing his fingers against her waist as he gazed at her with open adoration, a smile flickering at the edge of his mouth. "You know, I might just have to marry you."

She giggled, not caring if she sounded silly or too enthusiastic, and she put her arms around his neck and caught that lightning smile with a kiss.

The party was a whirlwind of laughter and stolen kisses. Henry's talks with his ex and his friends had gone better than expected. For all their pushing, most of them hadn't been quite as blind to Henry's clench-jawed resistance to the scheme as they may have seemed. Understandably, his ex hadn't wanted to stick around for the party, so she'd taken some of the group to town for the evening, where they'd managed to snag a late reservation at Mario's. The rest of their group were friendly enough whenever Annette and Henry encountered them, though—like Annette's friends—they mostly seemed to be trying to keep out of their way.

Annette didn't actually dislike the ones she met as much as she thought she would. Though she would've been hard-pressed to muster up antagonistic feelings toward anyone that evening. The whole world seemed full of hope and love and joy. There were very few moments Annette didn't spend holding Henry's hand or wrapped in his arms on the dance floor. She had his phone number, and they had already arranged two dates for the week they got back, and everything felt like it was falling into place.

A few minutes before ten, the band's guitarist announced the impending fireworks and the party-goers started arranging themselves near the huge windows, or slipping out onto the wide veranda beyond, where a few heat lamps had been strategically placed to help combat the cold. Annette and Henry stood near one of the heat lamps outside, the starry sky winking at them above the silhouetted pine trees.

"Aren't you going to be cold?" Henry asked, frowning slightly. "Do you want my jacket?"

Annette slipped her arms inside his suit jacket and tilted her face up to his. "I'm good."

Henry pressed a warm, slow kiss to her cheek as his arms went around her. "What are you thinking about?"

Annette breathed in a big breath of air that smelled of snow and pine trees and something like sweet potatoes roasting. "Just how happy I am. And how lucky I am. When I was driving up here the other day I didn't believe I'd ever meet a guy who would think I was funny *and* take me seriously. And then suddenly there you were, so much better than anyone I could have possibly dreamed up. And I know this probably sounds bad, but I'm so happy your friends dragged you up here so I could meet you."

He smiled and kissed her again, on the lips this time. "Well, that makes me feel a little better about being so happy you fell into that snowbank so I had an excuse to talk to you."

Annette grinned up at him as the first of the fireworks shot into the air behind the lodge. The golden sparks lit up his face and sparkled his eyes and the rim of his glasses. "Thank goodness for hellish cramps," she said, and she kissed him again.

Anyone might have thought her silly, to carry such unwavering conviction that this man in front of her was the man she wanted to spend the rest of her life with. But Annette didn't care what anyone else thought. She was falling in love with him, and he was falling in love with her, and the future was stretched out before them, full of possibilities and affection and joy. And what on earth could be so silly about that?

ACKNOWLEDGMENTS

Thank you so much for reading! I had a blast writing this short little '90s rom-com, especially since it gave me an excuse to listen to hours of power ballads from the '80s and '90s. The ones that ended up on loop the most were "I'd Lie for You (And That's the Truth)," "When Love Calls Your Name," (which, incidentally, was what I imagined Annette was humming on the stairs before she and Henry have their date in town) "Making Love (Out of Nothing at All)," "Where Does My Heart Beat Now," and "Kiss from a Rose."

If you want to see more of Annette and Henry, they also show up in *The Map to You*. Actually, the entire reason this story exists is because an early reviewer of *The Map to You* mentioned something about wanting a spin-off about how Kinsey's parents met and something just *clicked*. (Thanks, Janina!) I had no idea how much I wanted to write a cute '90s ski trip romance until I sat down to write this, and I'm so glad I did, even though it came out rather longer than I expected.

Big thanks to Jayne Davis and Melinda Perzy for critiquing this for me on short notice, and for setting me straight when my attempts to bluff my way through the skiing parts were wildly off-base. Shoutout to my mom for the encouragement and two rounds of proofing. Any remaining mistakes are entirely my own fault!

ABOUT THE AUTHOR

Rachel Stockbridge wrote her first novel at 12 years old—a goofy mess from start to finish that took her a year to write and proved beyond a doubt that she could do it. Since then, she's never stopped writing and has dedicated her career to pouring her heart out into every book she writes. In her free time, you can find her running DnD games for her friends, crafting, or editing other amazing authors' work!

Find Rachel online:
Instagram: @rachelstockbridge
Facebook: @rachelstockbridgebooks
Twitter: @rachstockbridge
Or sign up for her newsletter:
newsletter.rachelstockbridge.com/signup

ALSO BY RACHEL STOCKBRIDGE

NEXT STOP LOVE SERIES
Next Stop Love
The Map to You

SHORT STORIES
How to Win Staring Contests and Intimidate People

www.ingramcontent.com/pod-product-compliance
Ingram Content Group UK Ltd.
Pitfield, Milton Keynes, MK11 3LW, UK
UKHW042002230426
12048UKWH00009B/504